The Baby

John Burningham

CANDLEWICK PRESS
CAMBRIDGE, MASSACHUSETTS

There is a baby
in our house.

The baby
makes a mess
with its food.

We take it
for rides in
the carriage.

Sometimes I help
Mommy bathe
the baby.

The baby sleeps
in a crib.

Sometimes
I like the baby.

Sometimes
I don't.

It can't play
with me yet.

I hope the baby grows up soon.

Second U.S. edition 1994
First published in Great Britain in 1975
by Jonathan Cape Ltd., London by whose permission
the present edition is published.

Library of Congress Cataloging-in-Publication Data

Burningham, John.
The baby / John Burningham.— 2nd U.S. ed.
Summary: A little boy describes his feelings about the new baby at his house.
ISBN 1-56402-334-6
[1. Babies—Fiction. 2. Brothers and sisters—Fiction.] I. Title.
PZ7.B936Bab   1994
[E]—dc20   93-24277

2 4 6 8 10 9 7 5 3 1

Printed in Hong Kong

The pictures in this book were done in pastels, crayon, and ink.

Candlewick Press
2067 Massachusetts Avenue
Cambridge, Massachusetts 02140